PUFFIN

ALEX IN WO

Yvonne Coppard was born in Ruislip, Middlesex, in 1955, the fourth of five children. Before becoming a full-time writer, she taught in London, Plymouth and Ely, then worked in child protection with the Cambridgeshire Local Education Authority. Married with two daughters, Yvonne lives just outside Cambridge. She loves reading, cinema, swimming, gossip (though not the vicious variety) and old buildings.

Books by Yvonne Coppard

ALEX AND THE ICE PRINCESS
ALEX IN WONDERLAND
WHAT'S COOKING, ALEX?

ALEXANDRA THE GREAT

Alex in Wonderland

Yvonne Coppard
Illustrated by Jan McCafferty

PUFFIN

To Kody, Raichle and Indy, with love

PUFFIN BOOKS

Published by the Penguin Group
Penguin Books Ltd, 80 Strand, London WC2R 0RL, England
Penguin Group (USA) Inc., 375 Hudson Street, New York, New York 10014, USA
Penguin Group (Canada), 10 Alcorn Avenue, Toronto, Ontario, Canada M4V 3B2
(a division of Pearson Penguin Canada Inc.)
Penguin Ireland, 25 St Stephen's Green, Dublin 2, Ireland (a division of Penguin Books Ltd)
Penguin Group (Australia), 250 Camberwell Road, Camberwell, Victoria 3124, Australia
(a division of Pearson Australia Group Pty Ltd)
Penguin Books India Pvt Ltd, 11 Community Centre, Panchsheel Park,
New Delhi – 110 017, India
Penguin Group (NZ), cnr Airborne and Rosedale Roads, Albany, Auckland 1310, New Zealand
(a division of Pearson New Zealand Ltd)
Penguin Books (South Africa) (Pty) Ltd, 24 Sturdee Avenue, Rosebank, Johannesburg 2196,
South Africa

Penguin Books Ltd, Registered Offices: 80 Strand, London WC2R 0RL, England

www.penguin.com

First published 2005
1

Text copyright © Working Partners Ltd, 2005
Illustrations copyright © Jan McCafferty, 2005
All rights reserved

The moral right of the author and illustrator has been asserted

Set in 11.5/16pt Adobe Leawood
Made and printed in England by Clays Ltd, St Ives plc

Except in the United States of America, this book is sold subject to the condition that it shall
not, by way of trade or otherwise, be lent, re-sold, hired out, or otherwise circulated without
the publisher's prior consent in any form of binding or cover other than that in which it is
published and without a similar condition including this condition being imposed on the
subsequent purchaser

British Library Cataloguing in Publication Data
A CIP catalogue record for this book is available from the British Library

ISBN 0-141-31804-X

Chapter One

Putting on her elegant designer sunglasses, Alex Bond, Superstar, looks around the tropical island beach for a quiet spot where she can relax and recover from her gruelling world tour. A week in the sun with her famous friends is just what Alex and her personal stylist and long-time best friend, Rosie, need. They are hoping for a little privacy.

'Alex!'

Alex sighs. Is there no escape from fame?

'Alex! I said, have you seen my –'

I was rudely awakened from one of my better daydreams by Mum pulling the sunglasses off my nose.

– 'new sunglasses!' she snapped. 'Didn't you

hear me asking if anyone had seen them? And no, I won't let you borrow them on holiday, even for a teeny weeny little while.'

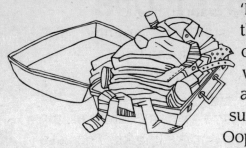

'I was only trying them on,' I said, offended. 'What would I want with an old person's sunglasses?'

Oops. That did it.

Mum pointed grimly at my open suitcase in the middle of the hall. 'Just get that sorted,' she said. 'It's time to go.'

The hall was in chaos – bags and cases everywhere. My little brother, Evan (the Terrible), was wandering around dressed only in his Superman underpants and eating an ice lolly, and Bear, our Newfoundland dog, was sniffing through all the luggage leaving a trail of slobber. Neither of them was exactly helping.

Mum was going into overdrive. 'Evan, get dressed. *Now!* And who gave you that lolly? Alex, get a move on. This should have been done last night . . .' and so on and so on.

Yes, the Bond family were once again

preparing for their annual holiday.

I pushed down hard on all the stuff in my suitcase and tried to zip the lid. 'The case is too full,' I said. 'I need another one.'

'No,' said Mum, still a bit grumpy. 'If it doesn't fit in that case, it doesn't go.'

When she uses that stern nursey voice there's no point in arguing. So I went for the big sigh instead and took out my hairdryer, my woolly jacket and my snorkelling kit. The case nearly closed.

'I'll do you a deal, Alex,' said Dad, who was sitting on another suitcase, trying to zip it up. 'Help me with this one and I'll help you with yours.'

He sat, I zipped, and we just about managed.

After a million years, we finally had the stuff packed and lugged it out to the car, where Dad began trying to work out where to put everything.

'Julie!' Dad called to Mum. He pointed at Evan, who was sidling towards the car with a guilty look on his face and dragging a holdall bigger than he was.

Mum came to investigate Evan's luggage. 'Evan, you were told to choose three toys plus

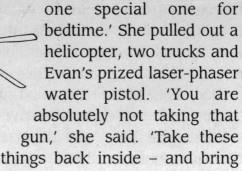

one special one for bedtime.' She pulled out a helicopter, two trucks and Evan's prized laser-phaser water pistol. 'You are absolutely not taking that gun,' she said. 'Take these things back inside – and bring the pyjamas and jeans and anything else you took out of here to make these toys fit.'

Evan pulled a tragic face and turned back with the offending items.

Dad leaned over the back seat to pack a cool bag on the floor. With superhero speed I took my chance to smuggle my CD player and entire stock of CDs into the car. But I wasn't quick enough.

'*N-o*, no,' said Dad, taking my player and CD

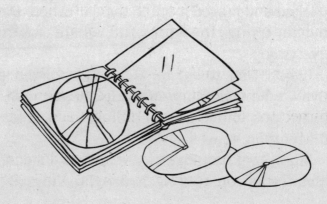

boxes from me just as I was about to slide them under the seat. 'Choose three CDs for the journey' and put the rest back. We haven't got enough space.'

'Dad, that's not fair!' I wailed, just as my best friend Rosie and her family arrived in their car.

They pulled up outside our house and honked the horn. Every one of them was waving and smiling, so we all had to stop being grumpy and wave and smile back.

Rosie literally tumbled out of the back of her car, revealing her big brother, little sisters and a huge number of bags stuffed in behind her.

'Hi, Rosie!' I called, and we hugged each other in excitement. We couldn't wait to go on holiday together. Next-door chalets at Wonderland Holiday Camp for a whole week!

Rosie was coming in our car for the journey to Wonderland, to keep me company and save me from a long trip with only Evan the Terrible for company.

I went over to the car and leaned through the window. 'Hello,' I said to Rosie's parents. I turned to the back seat. 'Hi, Josh! Hi, Megan! Hi, Daisy!'

Rosie's big brother, Josh, waved and smiled, and carried on rocking to his CD Walkman.

Her baby sister, Megan, thrust her dolly at me for a kiss and Daisy stuck out her tongue to show how pleased she was to see me.

Rosie's dad, George, was wearing the brightest, most flowery shirt I have ever seen. He's already big, but it made him look *huge*. 'How are we doing?' he boomed. 'Are you girls ready to go?'

'I think so.' I smiled. 'Just a bit of a problem finding room for everything.'

George laughed. 'That's what happens when your whole boot space is taken up with dog!' he said. 'I'll get out and give your dad a hand.'

'Thanks, George,' said Dad, overhearing him.

Bear was prancing around the drive, chasing his tail and sniffing at everything. Rosie's little sisters were laughing, which made him show off even more.

'Grab him, someone!' yelled Dad as he and George struggled to heave the big case on to the roof rack. Bear was weaving in and out of their legs.

'Come on, Bear,' I said, 'time to get in.' I patted the floor of our car boot.

Bear wasn't keen.

'Why don't you and Evan get in the car,' suggested Rosie's mum, Charmaine, 'so he knows you're going too.'

Evan and I went and sat on the back seat while Rosie patted the floor of the boot behind us. It worked. Bear jumped in, hanging his head over the seat, keen to see what was going to happen next.

The last bit of luggage was tied on the roof rack, the front door was locked. We were finally off.

'Show me the brochure again,' said Rosie, and I pulled it out of one of the bags.

'"*Wonderland, your world of holiday wonder*",' I read. 'Look at page fourteen – it's got a list of all the stuff you can do there. Beaches, sea, clubs – it's got everything!' I handed over the brochure.

'Fantastic,' said Rosie. 'We'll have to check out the Kool Kids' club first.'

'Definitely. No parents, no Evan, no hassle,' I agreed happily.

'But I'm going to the club as well,' piped up Evan. 'Mummy told me.'

'No, you'll have a different club – called Jazzy Juniors,' I told him. 'That's the one for little kids.'

'Oh, wow!' said Rosie, still reading the brochure. 'I didn't know there was a club for dogs too.'

'Puppy Pals,' I confirmed cheerfully. 'Bear can go there. It'll all be great.'

'So you won't be going to the club with me, then?' Evan asked me, frowning thoughtfully.

'No, Evan, I won't,' I said. *Aaaah . . . How sweet . . .* I thought. Evan obviously didn't want to go without me – and that was understandable, seeing what an amazing big sister I am. 'But Megan and Daisy will be there,' I added. 'And I bet you'll make lots of new friends too.'

'But you won't be there?' Evan insisted.

'No. Sorry, Evan, I won't,' I said, giving his hair a sympathetic ruffle.

'Oh good,' he said happily, and then settled back to look at his *Rocket Boy* Annual.

Charming.

At least *Rocket Boy* stopped Evan fidgeting for a while, though, and then he fell asleep. The rest of the journey felt blissfully Evan-free.

It wasn't slobber-free, however. Bear spent most of the journey standing up in the boot with his head poked nosily over the back seat. It was my job to wipe the steam and slobber off the back window with an old tea towel, so that Dad could see out. This involved shoving Bear's head out of the way and trying to reach across without making contact with his huge, wet mouth. Rosie generously took her turn too.

By the time we arrived at Wonderland and parked outside our chalets we were both covered in dog hair and slobber. But even a river of Bear slobber couldn't dampen our excitement. We were here! The holiday was about to begin!

Chapter Two

'First things first,' said Mum, stretching wearily after the long drive. 'A cup of tea.'

There was a general murmur of agreement from the grown-ups.

'Can Rosie and I go and look around?' I asked impatiently.

'Maybe you should wash first,' said Charmaine. She and Mum stared dubiously at our dishevelled and slobber-covered clothes.

'We can have a wash in the sea,' I suggested brightly. 'We came prepared. Ta-ra!'

Both of us pulled up our T-shirts to show the cossies underneath.

'Clever girls. You've travelled with Bear before, haven't you?' George laughed. 'But I don't think you should go in the sea without us,' he added.

Hmmm . . . .we obviously needed another cunning plan of action to escape . . .

Aha!

'Well, we could take Bear for a walk along the beach,' I offered. 'He needs some exercise, or he'll be a pain inside the chalet.'

'That's a good idea,' said Dad. 'A bit of a walk will work off some of his energy.'

'Off you go, then. Have a good time,' agreed Mum. Rosie's parents nodded and waved.

Rosie and I rushed off.

The beach was only a couple of minutes' walk away, and it was fantastic: golden sand, with some interesting-looking rock pools and big seaweed-covered rocks at the far end. It was quite crowded.

Bear looked out towards the sea – huge tail wagging, big nose twitching – taking in all the scents. He looked like he was in heaven. Suddenly he stood stock-still, his whole body tensed.

I knew that look. I followed his gaze and saw a toy boat bobbing about in the water. 'Oh no,' I groaned. 'Grab his collar, Rosie, quick!'

But it was too late. Newfoundland dogs are born to rescue things from water – and Bear had seen something that he thought needed rescuing.

He streaked off, wrenching the lead from my hand and sending me sprawling on the beach.

'What's going on?'

'What is that?'

'Aaagh!'

The squeals could be heard right up the beach as Bear thundered towards the water, splatting sandcastles, spraying sunbathers with sand, dragging towels with his paws . . . chaos everywhere.

Bear didn't even notice that Rosie was chasing him and calling him to come back. He was focused on that toy boat.

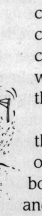

He crashed into the water, swam out, grabbed the boat in his mouth and swam back. He brought the toy to me and deposited it at my feet, waiting to be praised.

What could I do? 'Er . . . Good boy, Bear,' I

said weakly, patting him.

'My boat! Daddy, that dog's got my boat!' wailed a small boy. He pointed at Bear as though he were a criminal. Which I suppose he was, in a doggy sort of way.

I picked the boat up from the sand as the boy's dad thundered towards me, and noticed with horror that it was actually a remote-control boat, an expensive one. Luckily Bear hadn't damaged it – he has a very soft mouth when he's carrying out a rescue. But looking back at the trail of destruction he had made on his way to the water, I wondered if anybody would believe that.

'I'm so sorry,' I said to the man. 'Bear thought your boat needed rescuing . . .' I explained. 'Look – he hasn't damaged it.'

The man snatched the boat back and examined it. 'Hhrrmmm . . .' he muttered. 'Just keep that hefty great animal under control in future!' Then he took the little boy's hand and stalked off.

A little crowd had gathered.

'I blame the parents,' I heard a man say. 'What are they thinking of, sending two little girls out with a huge brute of a dog like that?'

Cheek! Poor Bear is not a huge brute – and

Rosie and I may be only ten years old but we're so sophisticated and glamorous, we're practically grown-ups! Well, almost, anyway.

I was going to put him straight, but Rosie pulled me away. We could feel people staring at us from across the beach.

'Great start to the holiday!' I muttered. 'This is so embarrassing. Let's get out of here.'

'It's all right,' said Rosie. 'Everyone will have forgotten about it by lunchtime. Let's go and explore the rest of the camp.'

Bear resisted leaving the beach at first – after all the excitement he wanted to stay and play.

'Come *on*, Bear!' I insisted crossly.

Looking a bit surprised, he began to trot along beside me.

'He was only doing what Newfoundlands do,' said Rosie.

'I know, I know,' I said. 'But sometimes he is just so embarrassing to be with. I think we should investigate Puppy Pals straightaway.'

We followed the Puppy Pals signposts to a fenced-off area right on the edge of the Wonderland beach. Inside there was a row of big kennels shaped like beach huts. Each one had its own little run and lots of doggy toys

and balls. Some of them
were occupied by one or
two dogs, who looked up
from their bones and balls to wag a tail in
greeting.

Bear was very excited, politely stopping to
exchange sniffs with all of them as we walked
past.

At the end of the row was a large enclosed
recreation area. A group of dogs was playing
in there with two Wonderland assistants in
uniform. They seemed to be having a great
time.

'It looks all right, doesn't it?' I said to Rosie.

She nodded. 'Bear will like it here,' she
agreed.

One of the assistants looked over and
smiled. 'Hi,' she called. 'That must be Bear! We
heard a Newfoundland was arriving today –
we're so excited to have him! Hang on . . .'

She threw a ball – and while all the dogs
rushed after it she came out of
the gate, shutting it carefully
behind her. By now, Bear had
his snout plastered against the
fence, keen to be part of the action.

'He looks friendly enough,' said the

assistant. 'I'm Jo, one of the Puppy Pals coordinators. Is Bear all right with other dogs? Is there anything we should watch out for?'

I grinned. 'Only the slobber.' I pointed to the long string of drool that was hanging from Bear's jaws. 'Watch out when he shakes his head – it goes everywhere.'

'Thanks for the warning,' said Jo. 'Now, do you think he'll be happier in the play park here – or in a garden hut by himself?' She pointed to the row of doggy beach huts.

'In the play park with the other dogs, definitely,' I said. 'He loves company.'

'Come on in, then,' said Jo.

Bear suddenly became alert – just as he had done on the beach before his embarrassing boat rescue.

I looked to see what had caught his eye this time. It was a small white poodle over in the corner of the garden.

As soon as Jo opened the gate Bear rushed past her and ran across to the poodle, with a joyful bark.

The poodle and Bear sniffed at each other – with some difficulty, since Bear is about four feet higher off the ground – and then the poodle started to get excited too. The two dogs

frolicked around each other.

'Your dog certainly makes friends fast.' Jo laughed. 'You'd think they knew each other already.'

'You would, wouldn't you?' I agreed. 'Actually, that poodle does look a lot like one he knows back home,' I added, thinking of Precious, the pampered pooch owned by my sworn enemy, Pearl 'Macaroni' Barconi. For one terrible moment I thought how awful it would be if it really *was* Precious – because that would mean . . .

'You're not thinking what I'm thinking, are you?' whispered Rosie.

I gave my head a firm shake. 'What would Princess Pearl be doing at Wonderland? With all the money they've got, her family aren't going to come to a holiday camp, are they?' I reasoned. 'No, she'll be sunning herself on some exotic cruise somewhere.'

'Yeah, you're right,' said Rosie. 'What a relief. Bear just likes poodles, I suppose – they say opposites attract. Look, the Kool Kids' clubhouse is right next door. Shall we go and take a peek while we're over here?'

I looked across at Bear. 'Bye, Bear,' I called. But he ignored me. 'He's not going to miss us, not while his poodle pal is here,' I agreed. 'Let's go.'

Everything was quiet at Kool Kids. 'I read in the brochure that there are no activities on Saturdays,' I said. 'Tomorrow is when the clubs get going.' I pointed at a board near the clubhouse entrance, where a strange-looking woman was pinning up some posters. 'The noticeboard should tell us what's going on.'

The woman turned round as we approached and gave us the hugest, brightest smile I have ever seen. Her hair was amazing – she looked as though her head was covered in yellow corkscrews. She had tried to control some of them with sparkly red and yellow hairclips, but they had sprung away from her head.

'Aha! I spy a couple of Kool Kids customers!'

she cried. Her voice was as loud as the trousers she was wearing – bright red and yellow with green-and-white parrots on them. She wore a baggy white T-shirt that said 'Kool Kids in Wonderland', and a sweatband saying, 'WOOFA'.

'Um, well, we were just going to look . . .' Rosie pointed towards the notices.

The woman stepped away. 'Wonderful!' she beamed. 'If you have any questions, you'll find me in the clubhouse. I'm Wendy, your Kool Kids WOOFA!' She said that last word loud and clear, leaning forward slightly. It really did sound like a bark.

Rosie looked at me. I shrugged. 'I . . . beg your pardon?' I said uncertainly.

Wendy laughed. The sound sort of ripped through the air. Think jet-plane take-off mingled with the last gurgle of the bathwater as it disappears down the plughole, and you just about get it. A couple of passers-by looked startled and hurried on. 'WOOFA!' she barked again. 'Wonderland Organizer of Fun Activities.'

'Oh, I see,' said Rosie.

'Wight, girls, I'll leave you to it – come and see me in there when you want to wegister.' She disappeared inside the clubhouse.

'Did she just call me a white girl?' whispered Rosie.

'I think Wendy has trouble saying her 'r's,' I whispered back. 'She must have meant *right*, girls.'

'Either that or she's blind,' replied Rosie.

'She asked us to wegister, remember?' I pointed out.

Rosie nodded. 'Things could get confusing . . . She seems nice, though, if a bit weird. Did you see her hair?'

'Awesome,' I agreed.

'The activities sound good,' Rosie said happily as we looked at the programme pinned to the noticeboard. She pointed to a poster next to it. 'What about the Miss Wonderland competition? Do you fancy yourself as a beauty queen?'

I shoved my glasses up my nose, tousled my hair and smoothed down my dog-slobber stained T-shirt and shorts. 'Sure, let's go for it,' I said. 'I'm bound to win – not.' I looked at Rosie and smiled. 'You'd win easily, though.'

'I'd rather put an earwig down my shirt than enter a beauty contest, thank you,' said Rosie. 'But look at this.' She pointed to another poster on the board. 'Friday night is Kool Kids' show night!' she read out. 'This week's production is *Alice in Wonderland*. First meeting Sunday morning, ten o'clock sharp.'

Acting! The bright lights, the fame . . .

'Yes! That's me!' I said. 'I mean, us . . .' I added hastily. 'We've just got to be in that, Rosie. We could turn out to be really great actors. We could be discovered – this could be it: our big chance to be famous!'

I'd always thought that Miss Westrop, our teacher at Derrington Road Primary, didn't really appreciate my talents. She'd only ever given me little non-speaking parts in school plays.

'Do you think so?' asked Rosie doubtfully.

'Definitely,' I replied. 'I just *know* that I could be Alice. Hey, I've even got the hair.' I pointed to my long, straight blonde hair. Well, nearly blonde – Dad calls it dishwater. 'And I've got a similar name!'

'Alex, tell me, how did you get started in acting?' the chat-show host asks.

With a wistful smile, Alex proudly hugs her three Oscars to her gold satin gown. 'Well, Michael, acting was my biggest dream . . .' she begins. 'Unfortunately, my teachers at school couldn't see the talent that was lurking beneath the gawky, speccy-faced kid . . .' She waves away the chat-show host's protests. 'It's true, Michael, I was gawky and I hadn't yet made specs totally fashionable again, like they are now. It was only by chance that I starred in a little holiday-camp production one summer . . .'

'Tell me all about it,' says Michael chattily. The camera moves in very close. I go for my biggest smile, but Michael is waving his hand across my face in a very distracting way . . .

'Earth calling Alex!' said Rosie in my ear. 'Time to go – we'll miss tea and my brother will scoff everything.'

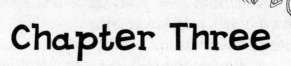

Chapter Three

The next morning Rosie and I got up bright and early – a bit earlier than we needed to actually, thanks to Daisy and Megan. Rosie's little sisters toddled, squealing, in and out of both chalets, 'helping' to get everybody up. Bear seemed pretty anxious to get out too, so Rosie and I took him to Puppy Pals, which was just opening up.

'Hello, Bear,' said Jo, smiling.

Bear wagged his tail and looked hopefully around the park.

'No poodle yet, Bear,' I said. 'Never mind.'

Rosie and I left Bear and made our way over to Kool Kids. Quite a few children had already arrived and were standing in a circle with Wendy in the middle, holding a beach ball.

Wendy turned to see us hovering at the

door. 'Hello, hello!' she cried. 'Come in, come in! Wonderful to see you! We're just about to start a little ice-bweaker game.'

Rosie and I hurried over to join the circle.

'I will thwow the ball to each one of you in turn,' said Wendy. 'Then thwow it back to me, saying your name at the same time, OK?'

It seemed simple enough, but when we heard that we had a Rosie, a Robert, a Rebecca and a Rhiannon in the group, I did feel a bit sorry for Wendy.

'Now, this time I'll thwow the ball to one of you and you thwow it to someone else in the circle, calling their name,' instructed Wendy. 'So Alex might thwow to Wee-annon, for example. And the twick is –' Wendy clapped her hands in genuine excitement – 'once you get the hang of it we'll start going faster and faster until we weally start to lose control. Oh, and –' she giggled with glee – 'we're also going to be wunning.'

'Wunning?' queried Rhiannon.

'Wunning,' confirmed Wendy. She ran a few paces to demonstrate, throwing the ball to Rosie as she passed her. 'Wosie!' she squealed just before she threw it.

Rosie caught the ball and started to run.

'Dominic!' she called, and threw the ball to short, dark-haired Dominic.

Everyone soon caught on and we joined in. The ball went flying all over the place. It's not easy to catch, or even throw, when you're running around trying to dodge people at the same time. But it was a good way to learn everyone's name.

Wendy had more fun than the rest of us combined, enthusiastically shouting out names and words of encouragement. 'Wachel! Wonderful catch. Oh dear, Alex. Wotten luck. Good girl, Webecca!' She dashed about like a puppy, chasing the ball whenever someone dropped it.

The game got fast and furious, and as other kids arrived and joined in, it became quite tricky to keep it going. When Wendy finally blew her 'Wonder Whistle' as she called it, we were all breathless and laughing.

'Wonderful,' she called, a bit breathless herself. 'That's a weally good start. Now, let me tell you what we're going to be doing here at

Kool Kids this week.' She clapped her hands with glee and did a little dance.

'Is she for real?' whispered Rosie in amazement.

I shrugged. 'Who cares?' I whispered back. 'Isn't she great?'

Wendy told us there were to be tennis matches, arts and crafts workshops and a treasure hunt. 'And all sorts of water activities,' she continued. She hugged herself with excitement. 'They're my favouwites – especially the waft building.'

I was catching on by now. 'Rafts,' I whispered to a puzzled Rosie.

'Oh, cool,' she said aloud.

'Then, of course, there is our gwand climax to the week,' said Wendy. 'Our dwama pwoduction, *Alice in Wonderland*!'

After a dramatic silence Wendy leaned towards us, as though she was about to 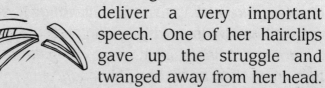 deliver a very important speech. One of her hairclips gave up the struggle and twanged away from her head. Wendy caught it with a swift, practised movement. 'But to be in the show you will need commitment,' she said very seriously.

'There will be wehearsals every day, maybe even *twice* a day later in the week, so that we can be weally sure of a wonderful pwoduction for all your families. So think hard about that, and if you do want to audition for a part, meet up here today at two o'clock sharp. We need an Alice, we need a White Wabbit, a Mad Hatter, a Queen of Hearts, a Cheshire Cat – oh, *lots* of wonderful, wonderful parts. Big parts, small parts, non-speaking parts – something for evewyone . . .'

Wendy was still talking, but I wasn't listening by then. There was only one part for me. Alice. It was my destiny.

The house lights come up to reveal Alex Bond – a lone figure in an apron and Alice band, bowing to the audience. The applause echoes like thunder; the audience is on its feet, whistling and shouting for more. Graciously, she beckons to fellow members of the cast to join her back onstage. They walk on and take their bows, but everyone knows that it is Alex the audience has come to see. Briefly, they share her glory and then creep away again, leaving her once more in the spotlight.

But as Alex turns to sweep graciously offstage, she sees that one member of the cast has stayed

to share her applause. Her smile dies on her lips as she recognizes . . .

'*Pearl Barconi!*' Rosie gasped. 'What are you doing here?'

Thinking it was just my daydream going wrong, I closed my eyes and desperately tried to change it. But no, my sworn enemy, the pampered princess of Derrington – Pearl 'Macaroni' Barconi herself – was here in this very clubhouse.

'Same as you two, I expect,' she said coolly. 'I've come to be in the Kool Kids' Show.'

'Ooh, do you girls know each other? How simply *wonderful*!' squealed Wendy. For a horrible moment I thought she would hug us.

'But . . . but you can't be *here*,' I spluttered at Pearl. 'This place isn't flashy or posh enough for you . . .'

'It certainly isn't!' Pearl said hurriedly. '*We* are staying at the Grand Royal Hotel next door! A friend of Amber's owns it, and Amber wants to help her friend bring a bit of Amber Barconi style to the place. Membership of Kool Kids is part of the hotel package. So I thought I'd come along and see what's going on.'

Pearl always calls her mum by her first name – Amber. It's one of the many annoying things about her. But then, I annoy Pearl back by calling her Macaroni, because her family's pots of money come from the pasta her Italian grandfather sold.

'And I'm so glad you did, Pearl!' beamed Wendy, who had been listening to every word. 'Imagine – the daughter of Amber Barconi in our little club. We're so-o-o honoured.'

And then Wendy actually gave a little curtsy. I thought I was daydreaming again, but no. Rosie was looking at her open-mouthed.

'Who's Amber Barconi?' asked Dominic.

Macaroni and Wendy exchanged one of those raised-eyebrow looks that happen when you're with someone who can't keep up.

'She was a *vewy* famous model,' said Wendy. 'Now she does celebwity shows and er . . . things . . .'

'Is she married to a footballer or someone else famous?' asked Dominic hopefully.

'No, of course not,' sniffed Macaroni.

'Oh,' he said, losing interest and wandering off.

I grinned and Pearl looked daggers at me.

'I've been a fan of Amber Barconi ever since I saw her in *Wags and Witches* years ago,' said Wendy.

'You mean *Rags and Riches*,' said Pearl.

'Yes, *Wags and Witches*,' Wendy agreed. 'I've followed her career, you know. I've got scwapbooks at home . . . but you don't want to hear about all that . . . do you?' she added hopefully.

We all looked somewhere else.

'No, of course not . . .' said Wendy regretfully. 'Anyway, back to business! I have a list of evewything that's happening here and I'll give each one of you your vewy own copy!' She made it sound like a piece of treasure. 'You can take it home and show your pawents . . . Will *your* mother be dwopping by at all, Pearl?' she asked, pretending to sound casual.

'I can ask her to, if you'd like,' Pearl replied smugly.

'*Could* you? *Would* you?' cried Wendy excitedly. 'That would be . . . oh, I don't know what to say. Yes, *please* . . . thank you!'

To spare ourselves any more gushing, Rosie and I took our lists and went outside.

Pearl followed us out. 'Wendy's vewy stwange, isn't she?' she said, with an evil grin.

'Shut up, Pearl,' Rosie snapped. 'We think she's great.'

'What would you rather have?' I asked

innocently. 'A small problem with the way you speak, or a big problem with all the stupid things you say?'

But even as I spoke, three of the girls from the club came outside and clustered round Pearl.

'Ooh, Pearl, you're not going, are you? We need you in the play,' simpered Rhiannon.

The other two girls – Amy and Rebecca – cooed in agreement.

Pearl looked at me with a smug expression. 'No, just getting some air,' she told her new fans. 'I fancy playing Alice. I'll be back for the auditions, don't worry.'

'You'll be great, Pearl,' said Amy.

'Well, it's a start. Frankly, apart from the Miss Wonderland contest –' She broke off and looked at me coolly – 'which I don't suppose *you*'ve entered?'

'No, of course not,' I said.

I was about to tell her why I thought beauty competitions were a really stupid idea when she cut me off by saying, 'Very wise.' Then she turned back to the others. 'Anyway, as I said, apart from the Miss Wonderland competition, the chance of a bit of acting is the only thing that makes this place interesting. It's only a little production, of course, but Amber started out in places just like this.'

'And look what happened to her,' said Amy breathlessly.

'Don't get your hopes up,' said Rosie loyally. 'Alex is auditioning for Alice too.'

Macaroni gave me one of her snooty glances and smirked. Then she flounced off – followed by the other three.

'I don't believe it,' I said to Rosie. 'Even here on holiday she manages to collect a fan club.'

'Incredible,' Rosie agreed. Her face changed. 'Oh!'

'What?' I asked.

'That poodle Bear made friends with . . .' she said.

'Oh, yuk! You're right,' I replied.

That poodle didn't just *look* like Precious – it really *was* Precious!

'But we've got more important things to worry about than Bear and his dodgy doggy friends,' I told Rosie. 'We've got to get ready for the auditions!'

Rosie and I decided that the pool was a sufficiently glamorous setting to discuss the auditions and our future acting careers. It was sparkling in the sun, and with the loungers grouped round the edge, it could have been a film set. There were two loungers free next to an older girl in a gold bikini and sunglasses; she looked like a model. Rosie and I slapped sunscreen on each other and settled down to talk about the show.

The paper Wendy had given us said that we didn't have to learn any lines for the auditions. But it also said that if we wanted to try for a particular part, then we should prepare a short scene with this in mind.

'I don't remember the story very well.' Rosie sighed. 'What parts are there where you don't have to say very much?'

I looked down the list. 'White Rabbit is the one for you,' I said. 'I think he just goes about looking flustered and saying, "Oh dear, I'm going to be late!" And other stuff like that.'

'I can easily do flustered.' Rosie grinned. 'Being *your* best friend gives me lots of chances to practise that!'

I gave Rosie a friendly shove. 'Right,' I said. 'So all we need to do is come up with a few flustered-type things for you to say – oh, and

 the White Rabbit loses his glove, so you can be flustered about that. And I'll practise Alice when she discovers she's shrinking . . .'

'Good idea,' said Rosie. 'What exactly happens, do you remember?'

I shook my head, frustrated. 'I wish we'd known what the show was going to be. We could have brought a copy of the story with us and been one step ahead of the competition.'

'Pearl, you mean,' nodded Rosie. 'Don't worry. You'll be miles better. And as you said yourself, you look the part. Pearl's too glamour-girl to be Alice.'

I gave Rosie a grateful grin. 'Thanks, Rosie,' I said. 'But you know how Macaroni has a way of twisting things to suit her. She'll have some trick or other up her sleeve. What can I do?'

'Let's just have five minutes of lying down and letting ideas wash into our brains,' said Rosie. 'Maybe some more of the story will come back to us.'

'All right,' I said, though I knew she just wanted an excuse to lie in the sun for a bit. Actually, so did I. The sun was so warm, the water lapped softly against the pool edge like a lullaby. Just five minutes . . .

'Tell us, Miss Bond, why do you always prepare for a role at the poolside? Is it some kind of ritual or superstition, perhaps?' the reporter asks.

Alex laughs and looks at the reporter over the top of her designer sunglasses. 'I suppose it is, really . . .' she replies. 'I prepared for my first ever part by a pool in a small holiday camp back in England. Nothing like this, of course,' she adds, waving a beautifully manicured hand towards the luxurious hotel grounds. 'But that little holiday camp called Wonderland was lovely in its own way . . . And then, after I'd won my first Oscar, I took Rosie, my personal stylist, for a short break on a tropical island – and discovered how good sunshine is for my freckles . . .'

She turns to the cameras and wrinkles her famous freckled nose. The reporters and cameramen are delighted.

'And what else did the White Rabbit say, Miss Bond?'

Alex peers at the reporter who asked the question. 'White rabbit?' she asks. 'Whose white rabbit?'

'Hello, anybody home?' Rosie asked, waving her hand over my face and tapping my nose. 'Come on, we've got work to do.'

We woke ourselves up by floating and splashing about in the pool, and then spreading out on the sunloungers to dry.

'OK,' I said, thinking hard. 'Alice is lounging about in the garden, and this rabbit comes by. And he's in a big hurry . . .'

'Why?' Rosie asked.

'Hmmm . . . Don't think it ever gets explained,' I replied. 'Anyway, he disappears down this hole and Alice – does she fall into the hole after him, or does she jump? Not sure. Anyway, she follows the rabbit down the hole for some reason.'

'Oooh, I remember now!' said Rosie. 'And then she goes all small, and then she gets bigger. Or is it the other way round?'

'Don't know,' I said. 'But then she meets the Cheshire Cat, who has a big smile, and he disappears bit by bit until only his smile is left. And isn't there a weird woman nursing a pig in it somewhere?'

'Oh yes – that's right!' Rosie beamed. 'And jam tarts, baked by a queen – and a prince who steals them,' she added. 'Yum! Fresh jam tarts . . . But what happens then? You know, we're not very good at this story.'

I stretched and turned over on the lounger, imagining the look on Pearl's face when it was announced that the part of Alice had been given to me. 'Don't worry, Rosie,' I said, 'I don't think it's going to matter. I bet no one else is going to know the story either.'

At least, that's what I hoped.

Chapter Four

We got to the audition in plenty of time. Pearl wasn't there.

'Perhaps she's decided not to bother,' said Rosie hopefully.

'More likely she's not nervous enough to worry about being late,' I replied gloomily.

'So, what part are you going for?' asked Dominic. 'I want to be the Cheshire Cat. My mum says I've got the biggest mouth this side of the Alps, and that I might as well put it to good use. Look!' He gave a huge grin, which seemed to cover more than half his face.

'Um, very good,' I murmured, not knowing what else to say. 'I'm hoping to be Alice.'

'You'll be lucky,' said Dominic. 'That posh girl has got it in the bag, I'd say.' He pointed behind us and we turned round.

'Hello,' said Macaroni.

My heart sank. She had done some serious preparation. Her hair, gorgeously glossy as always, was held off her face by an Alice band, and as for the dress she was wearing – well, it was almost like an Alice costume. Where had she found it at such short notice? There was no time to ask.

'Wonderful, wonderful!' boomed Wendy. She clapped her hands. 'So many of you wanting to take part. It's going to be one of the best shows ever, I just know it! Now, we'll start with Alice. How many of you would like to have a twy at the wole?' She smiled at Pearl. 'I can see at least one! Step forward, girls, don't be shy.'

Only Macaroni and I stepped up. Macaroni gave me a 'Why bother?' look and simpered prettily in Wendy's direction.

'Alex, would you like to go first?' enquired Wendy. 'Come and stand over here, poppet. And don't be nervous. Just take a weally deep bweath and be natuwal.'

I moved across the room to stand in front of everyone. Pearl folded her arms and fixed me with a mocking stare.

'I'm going to do the bit where Alice starts to shrink,' I said.

'Wighto,' said Wendy encouragingly, but Pearl snorted as though she thought I'd made a stupid choice.

'Oh no!' I began, giving my best horrified look. 'What's happening?'

Pearl sighed and examined her beautiful nails.

I threw my arms above my head. 'I'm shrinking!' I shrieked.

'Oh, honestly . . .' said Pearl.

I tried not to look in Pearl's direction, but my eyes insisted on a quick peep. She was making a big show of trying not to laugh, with her little fan club putting their hands over their mouths and exchanging looks.

'I'm really shrinking!' I shrieked again.

'I wonder if the specs will shrink too?' queried Pearl.

The fan club giggled.

Wendy half-heartedly put her finger to her

lips. 'Sssh. We must all have wespect for our fellow actors, mustn't we?'

But I could feel my face getting hot, and I knew it would soon be as red as a tomato. 'Oh no . . .' I carried on, 'I really am getting smaller and smaller . . .'

'And redder and redder,' added Pearl.

That finished me off. My voice sounded breathless and my face was burning. I just couldn't think of a single thing more to say.

'Um, wight, we'll leave it there. Well done, Alex.' Wendy started to clap enthusiastically.

The other kids joined in politely. You could tell they were wondering why on earth I thought I could be in the play at all, never mind take the lead. It was so humiliating.

'Thank you, Alex. That was . . . a vewy good attempt,' said Wendy kindly. 'Now, Pearl, would you like to . . .?'

Macaroni strode into my place as I slunk back into the crowd. She pulled a fan out of her dress pocket and waved it in front of her face. 'Dear, dear,' she proclaimed, 'how queer everything is today! And yesterday things went on just as usual. I wonder if I've been changed in the night? Let me think: was I the same when I got up this morning? I almost think I can remember feeling a little different.'

'Wow! She's learned the actual words from the actual story, I'm sure she has,' I whispered to Rosie.

How did she manage that?' Rosie whispered back.

'Somehow, she's managed to get hold of the book!' I said.

'But how could she have? There's no library here.' Rosie looked baffled.

'Sssh!' Wendy frowned.

'But if I'm not the same,' Pearl continued dramatically, 'the next question is, who in the world am I? Ah, *that's* the great puzzle.' She turned her eyes soulfully on the audience.

There was a moment's silence and then everyone applauded – properly this time. I knew I'd lost.

'Thank you, Pearl. That was *wonderful*!' cried Wendy. 'And vewy impwessive that you have taken the twouble to wesearch the part; well done. You have clearly inhewited your mother's gifts. Well done, indeed.' She caught my eye and added brightly, 'Both of you were vewy good. It will be a tough decision. Now, shall we do the White Wabbit next?'

In spite of my own gloom and despair I just about managed to give Rosie a little shove forward. She was so shocked by Pearl's audition, and so upset for me, that she made a brilliant flustered rabbit. The part was hers.

The next half hour went by in a bit of a blur. I was trying to shut out the sympathetic looks of the other kids and Pearl's cool smile of triumph.

'Wight, fabulous,' I heard Wendy say after a while. 'Let's have a short bweak, give us all a chance to get a dwink and go to the loo.' She beamed at us all. 'What a wonderful bunch of actors. It's going to be such FUN!' She clapped her hands on the last word and then waved her arms like a demented football fan. Another hairclip pinged.

'But just before we do,' she went on, 'I'll tell you who has the parts so far. I think for Alice it has to be Pearl. Such a beautiful Alice . . . And Alex was a worthy second,' she added hastily. 'So Alex, poppet, I'd like you to be Pearl's understudy for the part. Won't that be fun? Especially as you're alweady such good fwiends,' she beamed.

Pearl and I didn't look at each other.

'And Amy will be the Queen of Hearts,' Wendy added. 'Malek will be the Knave. And Wosie the White Wabbit, of course. So now we just need a dormouse, a Mad Hatter and the Cheshire Cat. We'll sort those out after the bweak.' Then she turned to me. 'Alex, poppet, why don't you twy for the Cheshire Cat?' she suggested, patting my shoulder. 'Not vewy many lines.'

She doesn't think I can cope with a speaking part! I thought miserably. But aloud I just said, 'All right. Fine.'

'Alex was distracted by Pearl,' said Rosie loyally. 'She's usually really good at acting.'

'And we need a weally good Cheshire Cat, so she'll be wonderful,' said Wendy kindly.

'But I think I'd make a good Cheshire Cat,' said Dominic, looking a bit put out.

'Do you, poppet?' Wendy said, sounding surprised. 'Mmm. Well, in that case . . .' She beamed at us. 'We'll have a gwin-off!'

'A gwin-off?' we repeated.

Wendy threw her arms round again. 'You can each have one minute to do your Cheshire Cat gwin, and the best and biggest gwin wins the part. What fun! But first, we'll have our bweak.'

*

'Cheshire Cat!' I said gloomily to Rosie as we wandered into the camp shop. 'I don't see this as the beginning of my acting career, somehow.'

'Everyone has to start somewhere,' said Rosie. 'And you never know, Pearl might break a leg or something.'

'No such luck,' I moaned. 'But I suppose it will be less humiliating than having no part at all.'

'Come on, be positive. Even film stars take little bit parts now and then – cameo roles, they call them. And they take them just as seriously as the starring roles.'

'You're right,' I said, cheering up. I could see myself as a Serious Actor. 'OK, Cheshire Cat it is. How about this?' I grinned at Rosie as widely as I could.

'Not bad,' she said. 'But let's do it the way a great actor would. Think yourself into the role. You're a Cheshire Cat. What does that mean?'

I looked at Rosie blankly. 'It means I'm a cat.' She had obviously forgotten we weren't at infant school any more.

'Yes – but you're much *more* than a cat,' said Rosie enthusiastically, throwing herself into the swing of things. 'You're a *Cheshire* Cat.

Now, breathe deeply and think Cheshire Cat. Feel that grin begin.'

I breathed in deep and pouted my lips ready to smile.

'Make it slowly grow . . .' said Rosie.

In my head, I pictured a semicircle being drawn on a big piece of paper and tried to copy the shape with my lips.

'And grow . . .' Rosie urged.

All Rosie needed was a folding chair with 'Director' across the back and maybe a baseball cap. But I could feel my grin getting wider and wider, stretching my mouth.

'Good grin!' said Rosie admiringly.

People turned to look and started smiling back.

'I think that's what they call an *infectious* grin,' said Rosie. 'Now let's go and make it work on Wendy!'

Back at the Kool Kids' club, Wendy decided I should go first. I took a deep breath, let my eyes go blank and went for it. I could tell people were impressed, and the applause at the end was much more genuine than it had been for my Alice impression.

'Now, Dominic, your turn,' said Wendy

brightly. But there was a sudden interruption when another WOOFA burst through the door.

'Can I have a word, Wendy?' she said, sounding out of breath. She looked very flustered. And her hair and sweatshirt looked wet.

The two of them went into a huddle in the doorway.

'She's from Jazzy Juniors,' Rosie said. 'I wonder what's going on?'

We edged a bit nearer, but it was hard to catch what they were saying.

'I think I heard them say "Evan Bond"!' said Rosie.

'I wouldn't be surprised,' I replied, rolling my eyes.

Wendy turned back to us. 'Childwen, I just have to pop over to Jazzy Juniors. I'll be wight back. Sukey here will play a lovely game with you in the meantime.' She dashed out of the door.

Sukey smiled at us nervously. 'Erm, right. Let's play a game, shall we?'

'What game?' asked Dominic.

'Erm, well, how about Oranges and Lemons?' offered Sukey 'The thing is, I work with the little ones,' she added apologetically.

'So I only know Oranges and Lemons, Ring o' Roses and The Farmer's in His Den.'

No one looked impressed.

'How about if we just talk amongst ourselves for a bit,' Rosie suggested sensibly.

Everyone else readily agreed and Sukey looked relieved.

I turned to Rosie, ready to practise my Cheshire Cat grin while we were waiting. But now she was looking *very* concerned.

'Uh-oh,' she said quietly.

'What?' I asked, confused.

'Look at Dominic!' she hissed.

Dominic was practising his Cheshire Cat grin too.

It was huge.

You could probably fit the Channel Tunnel into it.

'Well, that's it,' Rosie groaned. 'Sorry, Alex, but I think he's going to win. Look at the size of that mouth! Pearl will never let you hear the end of this.' She buried her face in her hands.

But I wasn't going to let Macaroni win that easily. I thought hard, looking at Rosie. And suddenly I remembered something. 'Rosie, I think I might have come up with a cunning plan,' I said calmly.

'Have you?' Rosie asked doubtfully.

I smiled and nodded. 'The Cheshire Cat has to be quiet and mysterious, right?'

'Right,' Rosie agreed. 'But so what?'

'So . . . if Dominic wasn't able to be quiet and mysterious, then he couldn't be given the part, could he? No matter how big his grin was,' I went on. 'And maybe something could make him laugh during his audition . . .'

'Ah! I see where you're coming from,' said Rosie.

I could see she was thinking hard.

'Nope, sorry – can't come up with anything that would work,' she said finally.

'Rosie . . .' I said, pulling a face as she looked at me.

'Oh yes! Gotcha!' she said happily.

Wendy came bursting back in, slightly flushed but jolly as ever. 'OK, thank you for waiting. You're such wonderful guys.' She turned to Sukey. 'Thank you, Sukey. Your little pwoblem is sorted now, I hope.'

Sukey raised her eyebrows and left.

'So here we go with our last part for the show,' said Wendy. 'Step forward, Dominic.'

Rosie moved away to stand at the back of the group.

Dominic started to smile, and I have to admit it was developing into a *huge* grin. But Rosie was about to go into action.

Rosie has this great trick she can do with her face. She moves her tongue across her nose like a windscreen wiper, crosses her eyes and moves her eyebrows up and down – all at the same time. It's gross – but really funny. And though nobody else was looking, Dominic was getting the full effect.

His grin slipped, then erupted into a laugh.

'Oh dear,' said Wendy sadly. 'I'm afwaid we can't wisk a Cheshire Cat who has a giggling fit, Dominic, poppet. We must give the part to Alex.'

I wondered if Dominic would tell on Rosie, but he was still laughing. 'I'll be something else,' he said. 'Something with not too many rehearsals – I want to join the surfing club.'

Wendy scribbled on her clipboard. 'That's settled then,' she said. 'We'll start tomowwow. We get five afternoons to wehearse. Wonderful! See you then.'

As we trooped out of the door, Macaroni sidled up to me. 'No hard feelings, I hope,' she said.

'No,' I lied. 'Actually, I think the Cheshire Cat

is a far better test of true acting ability than Alice. But how come you had a dress and a hairband so handy?'

'And how come you knew the actual words from the book?' added Rosie.

'Amateurs never understand the value of research,' said Macaroni with a superior smile. 'Amber knows the owner of the hotel. The owner of the hotel knows the director of Wonderland. So I knew all about *Alice in Wonderland* before I even arrived here.'

'That's cheating!' said Rosie indignantly.

'No, darlings,' drawled Macaroni as she swept away from us, fan club in tow, 'that's showbiz.'

Chapter Five

E ven though I had been given the part of the Cheshire Cat, I wasn't in a good mood after Macaroni's revelation. Rosie and I walked back to the chalets. But I wasn't the only member of the Bond family to have had a bad day. When Rosie's little sisters saw us coming they rushed over.

'Evan's been naughty!' Daisy said, her eyes wide with excitement.

'Ebban nooty,' agreed Megan as she toddled behind her, sucking steadily on her dummy.

Both girls stared at us, waiting for a reaction.

'What's he done now?' I asked.

'He's not allowed to go to Jazzy Juniors tomorrow!' said Daisy.

'Not lowd jazza joony,' echoed Megan.

'Why not?' Rosie and I chorused together.

Daisy drew a big breath, ready to give the big news. 'Evan took his water pistol to Jazzy Juniors and he hid by the fence

and squirted all the grown-ups walking past. And Sukey got cross and said "Stop it," and –' she could barely tell us the next bit, she was so shocked by the Jazzy Junior scandal – 'Evan squirted Sukey!'

'Sukey all wet,' giggled Megan.

'Then Sukey went to get the lady with the strange hair –' continued Daisy.

'So that was it,' I said to Rosie.

– 'and the lady with strange hair said Evan must go home. And he's not allowed to go to Jazzy Juniors tomorrow.'

'Evan not lowd. Evan nooty.' Megan toddled back to her toys, satisfied.

'Your mummy and daddy are cross,' Daisy

told me. 'Your mummy said she would throw the water pistol in the bin. Evan cried!'

'Poor Evan,' said Rosie.

'Poor Evan nothing,' I said, shaking my head. 'It will be that noisy flashing laser-phaser water pistol of his that he was told he mustn't bring. He must have sneaked it into the luggage.' (Actually, I was rather impressed by Evan's laser-hiding powers!)

'Evan the Terrible in Wonderland,' Rosie laughed.

She took her little sisters into their chalet and I went off to mine to get all the details of Evan's disgrace.

Evan and Dad were in the living room, looking glum. The laser-phaser water pistol lay on the table.

'I'm not allowed to go to Jazzy Juniors tomorrow. It's not fair!' whined Evan.

'You shouldn't have been so naughty,' I said. 'It serves you right.'

Evan smiled angelically. 'So we're going to the beach instead,' he said. 'All of us.'

I looked at Dad. 'What's he on about?'

Dad sighed and closed his newspaper. 'Your mother thinks that Evan played up to get attention. So she's decided we should spend more time together as a family. She's planned a family outing to the beach tomorrow. Rosie's family are coming too. A jolly, old-fashioned, family day out –'

'Oh no!' I said, dismayed.

'Don't look at me.' Dad sighed. 'I was looking forward to a quiet bit of fishing and some time to read, as it happens. But you know what your mother's like when she has a bee in her bonnet.'

Just then a stern-faced Mum came in.

'And it will be great!' said my two-faced dad, hurriedly changing his tune. 'We can all have a beach volleyball match, and er . . . explore the rock pools together!'

'But what about Kool Kids?' I protested. 'We're rehearsing a show, I can't just –'

'It's all arranged,' said Mum firmly. 'I've just been to see Wendy to apologize for Evan's bad behaviour. She told me that you and Rosie got parts in the show – congratulations, by the way – but she's happy to work around you not being there for a day. She said that most of tomorrow's rehearsing will be with Pearl Barconi, as she's playing the lead role.'

'Yes, isn't that a strange coincidence?' said Dad. 'Fancy the Barconi family showing up here the same week as us. I bet you were surprised . . .'

'Something like that,' I muttered. 'But, Mum –'

'It's all arranged,' Mum interrupted. 'We're going to have a lovely time. *Aren't* we, Alex?'

Humph.

The next morning, we all assembled outside the chalets for our jolly family day. All of us except Josh.

'Where's your brother?' I asked Rosie. 'How come he gets out of this?'

'He went out really early with the surfing gang,' said Rosie. 'He left a note saying he'd meet us later at the beach if he could. I bet he won't, though.'

'*My* brother will have to pay for this some day,' I muttered.

Bear was very excited to see everyone standing around together with bags and bats and balls – and, best of all, a picnic hamper. I

tried to tell Mum and
Dad that he should
go to Puppy Pals,
considering the chaos
he caused on the beach
before, but they were
having none of it.

'It won't be a family day
without Bear, will it?' reasoned Dad. 'It'll be
fine, don't worry. There are enough of us to
keep him under control if he gets overexcited.'

I agreed he had a point, so we set off.
Unfortunately the path Dad led us on took us
right past Puppy Pals. When Bear realized he
wasn't going there, he sat down and refused to
budge. With his size and weight, this was an
effective protest.

'Come on, Bear,' wheedled Dad, pulling his
collar.

Bear stayed sitting, firm as a rock.

'He wants to play with Precious – that
spindly little poodle that belongs to the
Barconis,' I explained. 'For some reason
they've become friends! You won't budge him
without a bribe.'

'Honestly, Bear, you do take the biscuit,'
said Mum.

At the word 'biscuit' Bear's ears pricked up and he sniffed the air.

Mum dug into one of the bags and pulled out a custard cream. Biscuits obviously beat true love. Bear followed the waving biscuit trail until we were well clear of Puppy Pals.

When we reached the beach, Rosie and I volunteered to take Megan and Daisy over to the rock pools, to get away from the grown-ups.

Rosie's little sisters are very cute and we had a good time helping them choose little stones to put in their buckets and hunt for crabs. Bear ambled along behind us, having a good sniff and being very well behaved. I let go of the lead, just for a second, while I was reaching across to lift a rock at the far side of a pool.

Luck was not on my side. At that very moment, Bear caught sight of something on the beach. With one huge, joyful bark he bounded off, trailing the lead behind him.

'Bear!' I shouted. We grabbed Daisy and Megan and ran after him, but there was no chance of catching up. All we could do was follow, apologizing to everyone for the trampled sandcastles, paw-printed towels and the sand sprays sticking to lotioned sunbathers.

Bear, meanwhile, had reached his destination and was joyfully prancing around, chasing his tail and nuzzling up to . . . Precious the Poodle. So she hadn't gone to Puppy Pals today, either. And if Precious was there, then so were the Barconis.

Great!

Not.

'Bear! Bad dog!' I shouted, grabbing his lead. But Bear had his beloved Precious at his side and took no notice of me. She was just as pleased to see him, and the two did a little dance together in the sand.

'I wish I had a camera,' Rosie laughed. 'They look so cute!'

But clearly Amber Barconi did not think so. 'Precious!' she screamed. 'Get that brute away from my Precious!'

Mr Barconi had been laughing too, but one

furious look from his wife put a stop to that and he dived in and scooped up Precious, who immediately started yapping and squirming to get back to Bear.

Amber pulled off her huge designer sunglasses and glared at me as I tried to pull Bear away. She looked outraged.

'I'm really sorry,' I said. 'I don't know what's come over him.'

Mr Barconi laughed. 'Summer romance, I'd say.'

'Don't be ridiculous,' snapped Amber. 'Not a pedigree toy poodle and a great big brute like that!'

'Newfoundland,' I corrected.

'Whatever. Alison, I took Precious out of Puppy Pals so that she wouldn't be mixing with the big, rough dogs,' Amber went on.

'Bear isn't rough!' I protested. 'And my name's Alex, by the way,' I added, for about the hundredth time since I'd known Amber.

Amber put her sunglasses back on and took Precious out of Mr Barconi's arms. Precious was still straining to get away and reach Bear, but Bear had at least quietened down a bit and wasn't jumping any more. Just being near to his darling was enough.

'Take that animal away, Alison, and we'll say no more about it,' said Amber frostily.

'Right,' I said. 'Come on, Bear. Leave little Poochpuss alone now.'

'Precious,' corrected Amber.

'Leave *precious* little Poochpuss alone now,' I repeated, and stalked off.

Or at least, I *tried* to stalk off. Bear didn't budge, and I fell over.

Tutting loudly, Amber marched off down the beach with Precious in her arms.

Bear followed.

Try as I might, I could not get him to leave the little dog's side.

Rosie took her sisters back to her mum and returned with Dad, who couldn't shift Bear either.

Giving up and looking very embarrassed, he turned to Amber. 'Um, look, I honestly don't think Bear will cause, er – Precious, is it? – any harm,' he said. 'Perhaps the easiest thing for the moment is just to let them play together, and keep an eye on them. Tell you what,' he added brightly, 'why don't you come and join us? We're going to play a bit of beach volleyball.'

Amber looked absolutely horrified, but Mr Barconi said, 'What a nice idea. We'd love to. Come on, Amber darling, stop making such a fuss and relax for once.'

Bear and Precious snuggled together for a snooze during the game.

Mr Barconi was surprisingly good at beach volleyball, but Amber didn't even take her shoes off.

'Go for it, girl!' Rosie's dad yelled as he thundered past her across the sand.

Amber tottered about, waving her arms and occasionally getting near the ball, but she never once hit it. She usually fell over.

Josh showed up when it was nearly time to go home and finished up the food, and then we all trooped back together towards the chalets.

Together, Dad, Josh and I just about managed to haul Bear into ours as the Barconis went off towards their posh hotel. We could hear Precious yapping all the way.

Rosie's dad chuckled. 'She's a character, isn't she, that Amber Barconi?'

Rosie and I exchanged looks, but said nothing. We went off to my room.

'Thank goodness that's over!' Rosie sighed, flopping on to the bed.

'Torture all round,' I agreed. 'But at least Macaroni wasn't there. Let's try and forget it. We have more important things to do.'

'Like what?' asked Rosie.

'We have to rehearse your role as the White Rabbit,' I declared.

'*We* have to rehearse?' queried Rosie.

I adopted what I hoped was a Hollywood director's accent. 'Sure thing, honey. I'm gonna make you the best White Rabbit Wonderland has ever seen . . .'

'Thank you – thank you all . . .' Alex Bond smiles as she cradles her Best Director award, surrounded by the grateful cast of her latest blockbuster movie. 'But my special thanks must go to Rosie Stevens – my best friend and personal stylist – who has been by my side since my directing talent was first discovered. Come on out here, Rosie.'

To polite applause, a red-faced, smiling Rosie comes up onstage and hugs her friend.

'As the world knows, Rosie and I started out as the Cheshire Cat and the White Rabbit in a tiny

holiday-camp production of Alice in Wonderland . . .' *Alex continues.*

Rosie wrinkles her nose, rabbit-like, and Alex gives a Cheshire Cat grin.

The audience goes wild. The TV cameras move in for a close-up to broadcast the moment round the world . . .'

'Alex, how's this?' *says the dinner-jacketed host of the ceremony. He raises his arms and flops his wrists, then sticks out his front teeth and screws up his nose and eyes.*

'I . . . er . . .' *Alex flounders.*

'Alex!' Rosie said impatiently. 'I said, how's this?' She flapped her floppy wrists about and wiggled her screwed-up nose. Then she made a chomping noise with her pretend sticky-out front teeth.

I sighed. 'We've got work to do.'

Chapter Six

Rosie and I were both keen to get back to Kool Kids the next day. But as soon as we arrived, it became clear that Macaroni had Wendy wrapped round her little finger.

'Excellent, Pearl, excellent,' Wendy murmured whenever Macaroni so much as raised an eyebrow. 'Your mother's talent weally shines thwough, poppet.'

'It's my own talent, actually,' replied Macaroni sniffily.

It was time to rehearse the scene where Alice meets the White Rabbit.

'I think I should be right at the front of the stage for this bit,' said Macaroni importantly. 'After all, the White Rabbit's just a dream figure, isn't he?' She looked at Rosie. 'And Rosie is a bit solid to play a dream figure. If we move her further back she'll look more dreamlike. Spotlight on me, shadow on White Rabbit. See what I mean?'

'Yes, I see exactly. That's quite inspired, Pearl,' cooed Wendy. 'Have you been discussing your ideas with your mother, by any chance?'

Pearl casually flung a lock of silky hair back from her face. 'Amber is of course very supportive of everything I do,' she said airily. 'But she believes in standing back and letting the creative spirit flow freely, rather than telling everyone what to do.'

Rosie and I both snorted. That was soooo not true.

Wendy and Macaroni glared at us both disapprovingly.

'It must be wonderful to have such an inspiwational pawent,' said Wendy. 'I do hope your mother is able to come along to our little performance on Fwiday . . .' she added anxiously.

'Amber's looking forward to it,' answered Macaroni graciously. 'In fact she was wondering about stopping by to see a rehearsal or two, if you'd like the benefit of her experience.'

'No, please, no!' I groaned.

Wendy either didn't hear or was choosing to ignore me. Her eyes lit up like Christmas tree lights. 'Oh, do you think she would? That would be wonderful, just wonderful!'

'I'll ask her,' said Macaroni smugly.

I looked round the group to see if anyone else thought this was a terrible idea. But Dominic and Malek were chatting to each other and hadn't been listening, and everyone else looked almost as starstruck as Wendy.

'So, on with the wehearsal,' said Wendy, clapping her hands. 'Pearl, poppet, are you weady for your scene with the Mad Hatter?'

Pearl gave a pretty little cough. She looked at Amy. 'Nearly, Wendy. I'm a bit worried about conserving my voice for the actual night. I just need a drink of water . . .'

'I'll get it,' chorused Amy and Rhiannon together. They both raced off, each determined to be the one that got to serve their idol.

'Um, if Pearl's got a sore throat, I can step in,' I volunteered. 'I've been learning the lines, just in case.'

'That's sweet,' said Macaroni in a pretending-to-be-kind voice. 'But let's face it – even with a sore throat I'm better than you.'

She sighed a dramatic sigh. 'No, I'll carry on.'

Amber showed up at the rehearsal the very next day.

'Oh, Amber Barconi! I can't believe it!' Wendy squeaked when Amber sauntered in. 'I never believed I'd meet you in the flesh!'

For a moment, I thought she was going to kiss Amber's hand, but she made do with a sort of little bow. She turned to us with flushed cheeks and an excited sparkle in her eyes. 'Isn't it *wonderful*, childwen?' she breathed. 'A pwofessional celebwity taking an intewest in our little show.'

Even Amber looked a bit surprised at the extravagance of Wendy's welcome, but she quickly recovered and put on a gracious smile. 'We all have to start somewhere,' she said. 'And who knows? I might be helping to nurture a great talent of the future.' She looked proudly at Pearl.

Then her gaze shifted towards me and took in my ketchup-splattered T-shirt, my hair falling out of its plaits (as usual) and my glasses, which had slipped halfway down my nose. I felt my face going red.

'Even those with no professional future can

benefit from a little help with style and presentation,' she said. 'Hello, Alison.'

Now I was embarrassed *and* annoyed. 'Hello, Mrs Barkingonly,' I replied politely.

'Barconi,' she said pointedly, and moved on.

The rest of the rehearsal was a nightmare. No one could move without Wendy seeking Amber's advice.

'I thought the White Wabbit should have a little wed jacket, so that he has somewhere to keep the pocket watch he keeps looking at. Or do you think he should just cawwy it? Oh, and I'd be vewy intewested to hear your ideas on the best way to show the pack of cards tumbling down at the end . . .'

Amber, of course, had an answer for everything she was asked and quite a few more things too. No one escaped her opinion.

She suggested my grin should not be quite as broad.

'But that's the whole point

about the Cheshire Cat,' I protested. 'There's nothing to him except the grin.'

'But such a wide grin is so vulgar, Alison,' Amber said sniffily. She looked at me critically with her head to one side. 'And it may be a trick of the light, but aren't your teeth a little crooked?'

'No, they're not!' I said hotly.

I checked my teeth as soon as I got back to the chalet to see which ones were crooked.

None of them!

'We can't go on like this,' I groaned that evening as Rosie, Josh and I sat together at the beach barbecue. Our parents were joining in the limbo-dancing competition, so we had been forced to find a spot well away from the action so that people wouldn't think we were related. 'Amber Barconi is spoiling everything. I don't even want to be in the stupid show any more.'

'I know what you mean,' agreed Rosie. 'But we can't pull out now. It would let everyone else down and that wouldn't be fair.'

'If only we could somehow get rid of Pearl as the lead,' I said dreamily. 'Then Amber wouldn't stick around. And the part of Alice would come back to me – cos it was always meant to be my part, really.'

Rosie grinned at me. 'Get rid of Pearl? There's an idea. But how?' she asked, twirling the straw in her cola.

'How about we find a couple of kidnappers and just let slip how much money her family have got and where her hotel is,' I suggested.

'How many kidnappers do you know, then?' asked Rosie.

'None,' I had to admit. 'Besides, I'd give it maybe an hour, two tops, before she drove them mad. They'd pay her family to take her back.'

'We're stuck with her, then,' said Rosie.

'Yep. And, worse still, we're stuck with her mother,' I agreed.

We sipped our cola in gloomy silence.

Suddenly, Josh spoke. It's so rare for Josh to say something voluntarily it was worth listening. 'You need a diversion,' he said.

'What do you mean?' I asked.

'Find something or someone that's more important to Amber Barconi than advising on the show,' Josh explained. 'Divert her.'

'Good idea, if we knew who or what that could be,' said Rosie.

Josh shrugged. 'Doesn't have to be real. Make it up.'

'He's right!' I shouted. 'That's brilliant, Josh!' I almost threw my arms round him, but managed to remember that he was a boy and stopped myself just in time.

'So, what does Amber Barconi care about most?' asked Josh.

'Herself,' I said. 'How she looks, I mean.'

'Being a celebrity and getting lots of attention,' said Rosie.

'Yeah, that too,' I agreed.

'That's where you have to find your diversion, then,' said Josh wisely. He obviously felt he had done enough, as he then fished out his CD Walkman headphones and disappeared back into his own world.

Rosie and I stared at the barbecue flames and the flickering shadows of the limbo dancers for a long time. But I got there in the end.

'I know,' I said. 'Nat Carlton.'

'Who?' asked Rosie blankly.

'He's a celebrity photographer,' I explained. 'He has lots of posh exhibitions all over the world. I saw him being interviewed on TV the other week. I wonder what Amber would do if she found out that Nat Carlton had been seen on the beach, wandering around with a camera . . .'

The next day, when Pearl was off in a corner giggling and being fawned over by her fans during a break in rehearsals, and Amber was fussing about as usual, Rosie and I started the conversation we had carefully rehearsed the night before.

'Ooh, Rosie, I forgot to tell you,' I said in a loud voice. 'I heard someone say that they'd seen Nat Carlton on the beach yesterday . . .'

'Wow! I wonder what he's doing here?' said Rosie.

Out of the corner of my eye I saw Amber edging closer. She pretended not to be listening but her ears were on stalks.

'They said he's got an exhibition coming up in London and he wants to find a woman to be "The Face of Summer" or something,' I lied..

'Why can't he use one of his glamorous London models?' asked Rosie.

'Well, apparently he said he's looking for someone a bit more interesting,' I went on seriously. 'A woman with more experience.'

Amber edged even closer.

'I don't know why he chose to come here,' I said, trying not to laugh. 'But anyway, he's going around the camp with his camera to see  what he can find. No one's supposed to know, though, because he won't use anyone who actually poses. He's just going to watch people as they move about naturally.'

'That's really interesting . . .' said Rosie. She didn't need to carry on. Amber was halfway out of the door.

'Amber!' called Wendy, distressed. 'You're not leaving, are you?'

'I'm just about to do one of my solo scenes,' wailed Pearl.

'Sorry,' said Amber. 'I've just remembered a pressing engagement that will keep me busy for the next couple of days. Pearl, darling, I'm sure you'll be wonderful – I'll be at the performance, of course. Bye for now!' And she was gone.

Despite Pearl and the fan club sulking because they couldn't show off in front of Amber any more, the rehearsal went really well. Rosie and I went back to the chalets very pleased with ourselves.

'Mum, Dad, guess what we did at –' I stopped. Something was up in our chalet. Dad was trying not to smile and Mum's face was red and angry.

'Bear's in trouble!' said Evan. He was clearly pleased to be pointing the finger elsewhere for once.

'Why? What's he done?' I asked, looking at Bear.

The dog looked back mournfully at me and settled his head on his paws.

'He's been thrown out of Puppy Pals!' said Dad, who looked suspiciously like he was trying not to laugh.

'It's not funny, Martin!' snapped Mum. 'First Evan – and now Bear!'

'But what did he do?' I asked.

Mum sighed. 'It's that blasted Barconi poodle again,' she said. 'Amber has taken her out of Puppy Pals because she claims the other dogs –'

'Meaning Bear,' interrupted Dad.

'Other dogs are too rough for little Precious. And now Bear misses her so much he's driving everyone mad with his whining and moping.

So Marlon, who's in charge of Puppy Pals, has asked us not to bring him. Says he's lowering morale among the other dogs.'

Dad burst out laughing and Mum glared at him.

'Sorry,' he said, 'I couldn't help it. Never mind, Julie. Look on the bright side. Alex hasn't been thrown out of Kool Kids.'

'Not yet,' said Mum. She looked at me suspiciously.

I was going to point out how unfair this was, and then I remembered the absolutely untrue story I'd spun a little while ago to get rid of Amber Barconi. I decided to keep quiet.

'Now, Alex, what were you going to tell us?' asked Dad.

'Oh, erm . . . I've forgotten. It's not important,' I said. 'What's for tea?'

Chapter Seven

It was Friday morning. Only one more rehearsal to go before our show. Rosie and I walked down to the Kool Kids' Club together.

'Are you nervous?' asked Rosie.

'A bit,' I admitted, 'but excited too.' After all, even as the Cheshire Cat, *someone* was bound to discover me and realize my future as a star actress!

'I know what you mean,' said Rosie. 'Hey, is that Amber?' Shielding her eyes against the sun, she pointed to a bench near the main entrance. 'It is!' Rosie grinned. 'She's still waiting for Nat Carlton to discover her as "The Face of Summer".'

Amber was draped across the bench with Precious snuggled cutely under her chin. It was a warm day and this was a holiday camp

– almost everyone was slopping about in shorts and T-shirts. Amber was wearing a brilliant-white trouser suit. Her hair had been blow-dried straight and sleek, her lips were bright red and her eyelashes looked like she'd glued two black caterpillars to them. She was smiling and saying, 'Hello,' to everyone that passed by.

'There's that strange woman again,' said a man near us. 'Who is she?'

'No idea,' said his friend. 'Do you think she's a celebrity?'

The first man laughed. 'I don't know, but she looks daft enough to be.'

Rosie and I giggled and did a high five, and then carried on towards our Amber-free final rehearsal. Instead of the Kool Kids' clubhouse, it was being held in the camp entertainment hall – where we would be performing the real show onstage that night.

The butterflies in my tummy began again as we arrived. 'This could be our big chance to be famous, Rosie,' I said excitedly.

Rosie rolled her eyes and grinned. 'What are you like, Alex?' she replied. 'It's hardly a London theatre, is it?'

'But you never know what will happen,' I insisted.

As if to prove how right I was, Pearl didn't show up for rehearsal. We waited twenty minutes, and then Wendy decided we had better start.

'We need Pearl in almost evewy scene,' she fretted, looking anxiously at her watch. 'But we can't wait any more. I'll wead Pearl's part for now.'

'Typical Pearl,' said Rosie. 'She probably thinks she doesn't need to rehearse.'

'No, something's up,' I said. 'She wouldn't miss an opportunity to be the centre of attention. Maybe she's ill.'

'Something involving lots of ugly red spots, I hope,' said Rosie. She hopped off to rehearse her part. We were using costumes from the Kool Kids' costume collection for this last rehearsal. Rosie looked very cute – and spookily like a cuddly bunny – in hers, although she said it was really difficult to walk in. I, on the other hand, looked like a girl with messy hair and specs wearing a cat costume. If only I could have been Alice . . .

But where *was* Pearl?

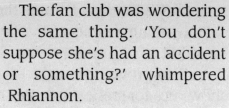

The fan club was wondering the same thing. 'You don't suppose she's had an accident or something?' whimpered Rhiannon.

'I'll go and look for her,' volunteered Rebecca. She looked at me and raised her eyebrows. 'It will be a disaster if Pearl isn't able to play Alice,' she said pointedly as she went off on her search.

Rebecca hadn't even left the hall when she cried out, 'Pearl? Is that you? It is! What are you doing over here?'

We all turned to look. In the shadows at the back of the hall, a few people were watching the rehearsal. Rebecca was standing next to one of them – someone covered from head to foot in a long-sleeved shirt, trousers, long silky scarf wound round her neck, a big floppy hat and huge sunglasses.

'Sssh! Go away!'

Yes, that was Macaroni all right.

Wendy clambered down off the stage and went rushing over. 'Pearl – is that weally you?' she asked doubtfully. 'Put the lights on, someone.'

'Yes, yes, all right, it *is* me!' Pearl snapped. 'Now just leave me alone.'

'Pearl, poppet, whatever is the matter? Why are you dwessed in that extwaordinary way?' Wendy asked.

'I don't want to talk about it,' said Pearl abruptly.

'Hey, you haven't visited the tattoo parlour, have you?' asked Dominic excitedly.

'No, of course not!' replied Pearl impatiently. 'I'm hiding from Amber – she doesn't know what I've done – Oh!' Pearl clearly thought she'd said too much.

Rosie and I looked at each other, eyebrows raised.

'What *have* you done, Macaroni?' I asked.

I didn't want to be interested, but I just couldn't help it.

Now they'd realized it really was Pearl, the fan club gathered round as if to screen her from my wickedness.

'Come on, it can't be so vewy bad, poppet,' said Wendy gently. 'We're all fwiends here.' She gave me a stern look. 'And we will do our best to help you, whatever the pwoblem is.'

Slowly, Pearl took her hands out of her pockets. They were a very strange colour. She started to unwind her scarf. Her neck was a strange colour too. Then she undid the coat and took off the hat and sunglasses.

Pearl's face, neck, arms and legs had gone the weirdest mud-to-orange mixture of colours you could imagine.

'Oh no!' gasped the fan club.

'Whoa!' Dominic laughed.

Wendy silenced him with a look. 'Oh, Pearl . . .' she breathed. 'It's fake tan, isn't it?'

Pearl nodded miserably. 'It's Amber's,' she said. 'She uses it all the time – but it always goes nice and even on her – and I look like –'

'An orange zebra!' finished Dominic.

'Yes, thank you, Dominic!' Wendy snapped.

'Macaroni, how much did you use?' I asked.

'Just a little bit at first,' said Pearl defensively. 'But it wasn't working, so I used a bit more.' She sniffed. 'And then a bit more.'

'It takes time to work, you idiot,' said Rosie. 'You're supposed to wait. Even I know that and I've never used the stuff in my life. *And* you're supposed to put it on evenly. Didn't you read the instructions?'

'I was in a hurry, all right?' said Pearl angrily. 'It's the Miss Wonderland contest this afternoon and some of the other contestants have been here a week longer than me, preparing and sunning themselves.' She made it sound as though her rivals had spent the whole week deliberately getting an unfair head start on her. 'So I thought . . .' She pointed to the unfortunate mess of colour all over her. 'But it's a disaster. I can't enter the competition now. And there's no way I can play Alice tonight, either. Now will you please just go away and leave me alone!'

'But, Pearl, we need you . . .' started Wendy. 'Without you, we'll have to hand over to Alex . . .' She looked at me and then added hurriedly, 'who will, of course, do a splendid job, but –'

'I'm not going to stand up there and have

everyone laugh at me!' Pearl replied sulkily.

A sudden shriek startled us all and we turned round to see Amber framed in the doorway. She stared at Pearl with a wild expression. 'Pearl! What on earth have you done?' she gasped.

'I thought it would look nice for the Miss Wonderland contest,' Pearl muttered, not meeting her mother's eyes.

'It's a disaster!' wailed Amber. 'Whatever possessed you to use fake tan without my expert advice?'

'I had the idea while you were at the hotel beauty parlour and I didn't want to wait,' Macaroni admitted miserably.

'Well, now look at you!' Amber said. 'You've ruined any chance of winning the Miss Wonderland title.'

'Perhaps Pearl could enter the fancy-dress competition instead,' I suggested. 'I mean, she could go as a pumpkin princess or something . . .'

Amber sniffed, then turned her back on me and grabbed Pearl's elbow. 'Put that scarf and those sunglasses back on, for goodness' sake, so nobody sees you on the way back to the hotel,' she told Pearl.

'I'm sure a good long soak in the bath will help get wid of it,' Wendy said hopefully. 'Maybe with a bit of hard scwubbing?'

'I am afraid not,' Amber said curtly. 'I use this brand of tanning lotion because of its extra staying power.'

'Well . . . never mind!' said Wendy brightly. 'Perhaps we can wite the whole thing into the scwipt. Alice could swallow a potion that makes her look . . . owange and –' Wendy swallowed hard – 'stwipy . . .' she finished on a squeak.

Mother and daughter flounced off together.

'Oh dear, oh dear . . .' said Wendy, anxiously wringing her hands. 'We've lost our star!' She looked at us in despair for a moment, and then said bravely, 'Alex, go and change out of that cat costume. You will be Alice tonight, and Dominic will be the Cheshire Cat. You know what they say: the show must go on!'

Chapter Eight

'*I always knew that my moment would come, of course. It was just a matter of waiting for it to arrive,*' Alex tells the star-struck chat-show host. '*Yes, my first starring role seemed like destiny. I was understudy in a small production down on the coast. And at the last moment I had to step in to save the show.*'

Alex gives the host a bitter-sweet smile. 'I was, of course, so very sad that it had to be at the expense of poor, poor Maca– Pearl Barconi . . . What? You've never heard of her?'

'Alex, get a move on.' Rosie was yanking at my cat costume's head, trying to get it off. 'Everybody's waiting to start the rehearsal.'

'Wighto, evewyone, let's make a start,' called Wendy, clapping her hands. 'Alice, you are the first on . . .'

Rosie gave me a thumbs up. The fan club looked on miserably, certain that the show was doomed without Pearl.

But the rehearsal went like a dream – a good one! I remembered all my lines and all the moves – and I didn't even feel nervous! Rosie managed to hide her nerves and was a brilliant White Rabbit. And apart from Dominic stopping to scratch his neck halfway through a major grin (Wendy cut the label out of his costume and after that he was fine), everything went without a hitch.

'Bwilliant! Bwilliant!' Wendy shouted at the end. She clapped her hands madly, her face flushed with excitement. The parents who had come in to watch at the back of the hall applauded too. A couple even cheered.

'Well done, Alex!' beamed Wendy. 'No one would know you'd stepped in at the last minute!'

After taking off our costumes, Rosie and I dashed back to the chalets to tell our families the news about my promotion to star status.

Everyone was delighted and, after lunch, when it was decided we'd all go down to the beach for one last afternoon together, Rosie and I didn't even mind.

Not until we saw the Barconi family sitting there, that is.

'Oh no,' I moaned. 'Get Bear to look the other way, quick!'

No such luck. Bear spotted Precious in an instant and pulled insistently on the lead until we took the direction he wanted.

'Ah, hello!' called Mr Barconi. 'How lovely to see you again. Please, do join us.'

From behind her huge sunglasses I could feel Pearl's eyes willing me to go away.

'Thank you, we will,' said Dad.

Rosie and I rolled our eyes at each other.

Everyone dumped their bags, pulled out the beach mats and started marking out their territory next to the Barconis. Bear and Precious were delighted.

'We were all so sorry to hear about Pearl's er . . . accident,' said Mum politely. 'I hope you're feeling all right?' she asked Pearl.

Pearl looked the other way.

'Take no notice of her,' said Mr Barconi comfortably. 'She's in a sulk.' He shook his head and patted Bear affectionately.

There was an audible tut from Amber, and then she slid gracefully off her sunlounger and pulled Precious away from Bear. 'I'm going to hire a pedalo for a while,' she said, pointing to the little boats being pedalled back and forth near the shore. 'And I'm taking Precious with me.'

She turned to Mum. 'I'd be grateful if you could prevent your . . . dog from following us.'

'Of course,' said Mum crisply. She used her best stern voice. 'Bear, *sit*! *Stay!*'

Bear looked her in the eye and contemplated disobeying, but then he sat down again with a whimper. Very wise.

As Amber tottered off in her silly high-heeled flip-flops that aren't actually meant to be worn in the sand, she turned to Mr Barconi. 'Antonio, if you spot *anyone* who looks even *remotely* like Nat Carlton coming along, raise the alarm,' she instructed.

Mr Barconi grinned and gave her a salute. 'Yes, ma'am!' he joked.

'Is the poodle going to help pedal the boat?' asked Rosie's dad, roaring with laughter. Everyone else grinned. Rosie's dad has that kind of laugh.

Everyone except Pearl. She huddled there, covered from head to foot, only her orange chin and scowling mouth visible as she stared out to sea behind her huge sunglasses.

Evan went over to Pearl. 'Can I just have one little look at the stripes?' he asked.

Pearl turned her back on him.

Bear sat there, staring mournfully out to sea at Amber's pedalo, which was now quite a way out. Precious was at her side, staring at the beach – looking for Bear.

Charmaine laughed and gave Bear a sympathetic pat. 'Poor Bear – his beloved has gone away to sea.'

While Mum and Charmaine settled down to read their books, the three dads started talking about football. Pearl sat there like a tragic film queen, saying nothing.

Rosie and I decided to help Evan, Megan and Daisy build a large sandcastle. We were just about to start on the moat when we heard a scream and a splash.

'Help! Help me, someone! She's fallen overboard and I can't swim!'

It was Amber's voice. She was standing in the pedalo and a little white shape was bobbing in the water.

Bear was instantly up and off, thundering towards the water.

'Help! Someone save my Precious!' screamed Amber again.

Mr Barconi was also running down to the sea, followed by an orange stripy Pearl-like blur.

Bear was ahead of them both. Calmly, steadily, he swam out to Precious, hooked her collar with his teeth and turned for the shore.

'Get that brute away from my dog!' screamed Amber.

'That's a Newfoundland, that is, love!' called a man paddling with his baby on the shoreline. 'Rescue dog. Leave him to it.'

Bear brought Precious to shore and laid her gently down on the sand. With her woolly white coat wet and slick she looked even tinier. Bear bent down and gave her face a tender lick. A moment later, Precious jumped up, shook herself thoroughly and gave a happy little bark.

There was a spontaneous round of applause and calls of 'Well done!' and 'Good dog!' and 'What a sight!'

Bear lapped it up and looked around

 expectantly. Sure enough, a little girl rushed up to give him a fairy cake.

Mr Barconi and Pearl reached the pedalo together and pulled it back in between them. Amber seemed too stunned to help.

'What a magnificent dog!' declared Mr Barconi as they reached the shore.

Amber hopped out of the pedalo and hurried over to scoop Precious up and shower her with kisses. 'Never mind, Mummy's here now. All over now. Poor little Precious . . .'

'She's quite safe, Amber, darling – thanks to Bear,' said Mr Barconi pointedly.

'What? Oh . . . yes.' Amber gave Bear a quick pat on the head – not enthusiastically, but at least she made an effort. 'Yes, er, good dog,' she said reluctantly.

'I am going to find the biggest burger on the beach for that dog!' announced Mr Barconi. 'That dog is a hero!' He set off for the burger bar.

'Oh, my poor nerves,' Amber went on. 'That was quite a trauma, wasn't it, Pearl?'

Everyone turned to gaze at Pearl – and got the shock of their lives. In all the drama, nobody had taken a proper look at her. But now, having peeled off her coat without thinking to rush into the sea, Pearl was standing there in her cossie, her disastrous fake tan on full display.

'Wow!' said Evan loudly. 'You look even worse than the Slime Monster in my comic!'

Evan's voice (and Pearl's orange glow) attracted the attention of even more people nearby.

'That poor girl,' murmured a woman. 'What a terrible affliction.'

'What *is* that?' asked a boy.

'Yuk!' said his friend. 'I don't know, but I hope it's not catching.'

'I can't stand this another minute!' Pearl wailed. 'I want to go home! I want to go home right now!'

She grabbed her coat and stomped off up the beach.

And that was the last we saw of Pearl in Wonderland.

Chapter Nine

L ate that afternoon, Rosie and I prepared for the show.

'I don't need to do much,' said Rosie. 'Most of my head is covered by the make-up and rabbit costume.'

So we spent most of the time trying to make me look like Alice – which was mainly Rosie spraying my hair with half a bottle of Mum's hair-thickening lotion and drying it straight and bouncy. Rosie is brilliant at making people look good, even when they've got freckles, glasses and straggly hair like mine.

'We are the biz, as Dad says,' announced Rosie with satisfaction.

I looked into the mirror. 'Wow! You've made my hair look brilliant!' I said.

Rosie grinned. 'Now, we just have to put

some eye make-up on so you look good under the lights. Don't worry, Mum showed me what to do . . .'

Film star Alex Bond takes a deep breath and settles back into the soft leather chair in front of her dressing-room mirror. Rosie, her personal stylist, reaches for her make-up kit. Alex tries to relax, but it's hard to – she's so excited. Who would have thought that the Queen would decide to attend the premiere of Dream Girl, *Alex's latest movie? And bring with her the American president, who happens to be here in Britain on a state visit? Today's newspapers have talked about nothing else, and Alex knows there will be a sea of flashing camera lights and an army of journalists fighting to get near her as soon as she steps out of the limo on to the red carpet outside London's most glamorous cinema . . .*

'There, that's it,' says Rosie. She stands back

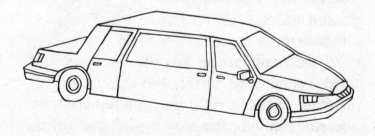

and looks at Alex's face very carefully. 'Yep, I'm really pleased with that. You have such an easy face to work with, Alex.'

'Thanks, Rosie. Great job,' Alex replies.

There is a knock on the dressing-room door.

'Shouldn't you be going, girls?' a voice calls.

Alex feels another little thrill of excitement. The limousine must be waiting for them outside . . .

Dad poked his head round the bedroom door. 'Girls! I said, shouldn't you be going? Look at the time.'

'Oh no!' gasped Rosie, glancing at her watch.

Rosie and I had been having such a good time that we hadn't kept an eye on the clock.

We rushed out of the chalet, shouting, 'See you all there!' and across the campsite to the hall. We arrived completely puffed out.

Wendy was at the door, quivering with anxiety – most of her hairclips had already pinged off. 'Oh, thank goodness!' she said when she saw us.

'We're really sorry, Wendy. We forgot the time,' I said.

'Never mind, never mind, you're here now,' she said, leading the way to the back of the stage. 'I've laid your costumes out weady for you. Get them on as quickly as you can and make your way to the side of the stage. I've got to go and introduce the show.' And then she charged off.

The fan club rolled their eyes at each other.

'I knew this would happen,' said Rebecca.

'That's what you get when you work with amateurs,' added Rhiannon.

Rosie and I ignored them and began helping each other into our costumes.

A round of applause started up and then we heard Wendy shouting enthusiastically across the hall.

'What a gweat pwivilege it has been to work with all your wonderful childwen,' she gushed. 'They have all wehearsed so hard this week. Some of you may have heard about the unfortunate event wegarding our leading lady –'

There was a rumble of laughter around the hall.

'But our wonderful cast just cawwied on, like the twoopers they are!' Wendy cried happily. 'Now without any more ado, let's open the show. Welcome to Wonderland's pwoduction of –' there was a pause and then a roll of drums – '*Alice in Wonderland*!' screamed Wendy.

The nightclub band, which had been roped in for the performance, struck up the opening music. In about two minutes the curtains would go back and the show would begin.

I couldn't resist peeping round the edge of the curtain. The lights were up and the hall was full – too full to spot my family, or Rosie's, among the crowd.

Until that moment, I had felt nothing but excitement at the thought of going out onstage in front of a big audience. This was my big chance, after all. Superstar Alex Bond's first step to fame!

But now, as I stared out at the sea of strange faces looking expectantly at the stage, there seemed to be something very tight wound round my chest. I could hardly breathe.

And my mind went a complete blank.

Chapter Ten

I clasped Rosie fearfully. 'I can't remember any of my lines!' I hissed frantically. 'I can't do it, Rosie. I can't go on. Quick! Get the understudy!'

'You are the understudy,' Rosie hissed back.

'I can't do it!' I repeated. My face was burning like a hot coal, but I felt cold with panic.

'You'll be fine, Alex, honestly. Come on,' said Rosie. 'I'm the one who's supposed to get nervous, not you!' She nudged my shoulder playfully.

But I wasn't feeling playful. 'It's all right for you – you can hide in your costume,' I said. 'Everyone's going to be staring at me! Macaroni was right,' I whimpered. 'I don't even look like Alice. Remember what she said? You can't have an Alice in Wonderland wearing glasses. What am I going to do?'

Rosie turned and stared at me. I could tell she was thinking hard. Then she grabbed my arms and gave me a little shake. 'Maybe Macaroni *was* right about the glasses thing . . .'

'W-what?' I stammered. As if things weren't bad enough, my best friend was joining my worst enemy to put the boot in!

Rosie suddenly whipped off my glasses and stowed them in her rabbit costume pocket. 'Look at the audience now,' she ordered.

I peeped round the curtain again.

This time, I faced a multicoloured blur that could have been anything. It certainly didn't look like a crowd of people. I felt the band round my chest loosen. I could breathe again.

'Now, let's get going before you have a chance for another wobbly!' hissed Rosie. As the curtains parted, she pushed me onstage.

And suddenly everything came back to me in a rush.

I turned to face Rosie. 'A white rabbit with a pocket watch? How extraordinary!' I began. 'Hey there! White Rabbit! Won't you stay a while and talk to me?'

'Only if you look at me when you speak,'

said the White Rabbit – from behind me.

The audience were laughing.

I squinted hard at what I'd been talking to. It was a cardboard tree.

Good old Rosie. Her quick thinking had saved me. The audience thought my not being able to see was a deliberate part of the show!

There were just a few other disasters along the way.

At the Mad Hatter's tea party, I sat on the chair next to him – and crushed his hat.

'You'll have to buy a new one, you know,' Robert said crossly. 'That'll be one million pounds, please.'

The audience roared with laughter.

And when it was time for me to pour the tea, I spilled it all over the dormouse instead of into the cups.

Without turning a dormouse hair, Joe licked at his fur and said, 'Mmmm. I think I'll have some sugar with that, please.'

There was another roar of laughter and a round of applause.

When we took our final bow, the audience clapped and whistled and cheered like mad. It was fantastic. I could have stayed there forever.

'You were all wonderful! Wonderful!' cried Wendy, coming up onstage.

'Everyone look over here, please!' called the camp photographer from the front of the audience.

'Ah yes,' beamed Wendy. 'We need pictures of you all for our Wonderland Wall of Fame.'

After the photos had been taken, the audience began to troop out and we all made our way backstage to change out of our costumes.

'Before evewyone leaves, I have one more surpwise for you . . .' said Wendy, her smile even wider than usual, and her cheeks flushed with excitement. 'It was a huge surpwise to me too, let me tell you. But in the audience tonight, watching the whole show was –' you could almost hear the drum roll going on in Wendy's head as she made the most of the announcement – 'Kimberley Hunter!'

'Who?' said Dominic loudly.

But everyone else gasped. Kimberley Hunter, the movie star – here! It didn't seem possible.

'Kimberley used to be one of our WOOFAs, before she got her first film wole and went on to fame and fortune,' Wendy told us proudly. 'She's been filming her latest movie locally and popped into Wonderland on a visit down memowy lane, as they say. Isn't that exciting?' She did her little arm wave. 'And guess what?' she went on. 'Kimberley wants to meet you all!' Her two remaining hairclips pinged off as if they couldn't contain their amazement.

And then suddenly I saw a tall fuzzy figure walking towards us. I reached for my glasses and put them on.

It *was* Kimberley! I felt as though I was in one of my daydreams. But no, she really was standing there!

'Hi, everyone!' she said. 'You were all so great tonight! It's been a real thrill to return here, where it all began for me.'

And then she smiled straight at me. 'Alex, you were wonderful. You're a natural comedian. I haven't laughed so much for ages.'

I looked at Rosie and winked. If only Kimberley knew!

'I expect to see you in Hollywood one day,'

Kimberley added. 'Make sure you look me up, eh?'

Yes, a real live film star asked me to look her up when I arrived in Hollywood!

Kimberley then signed photographs for us all.

'Can you put, *To my lovely boyfriend, Dominic Hardy*?' asked Dominic as he thrust his photo up for Kimberley to sign.

'Didn't I overhear you asking who I was?' asked Kimberley, grinning widely at him.

'I know, but I bet my big brother will fancy you – so he'll be dead jealous,' said Dominic happily.

Everyone said their goodbyes and began to make their way out.

'Excuse me . . . excuse me . . . can we get through, please!'

Two men, one with an impressive-looking camera and the other with a notebook, pushed their way through the crowd.

'Kimberley, good to see you again. Phil Watts, from *Hiya!* magazine's celebrity-spotter page . . .' the one with the notebook said.

Kimberley took the outstretched hand with a smile, but she didn't look as if she remembered him at all. 'Ah, Phil, lovely to see you again,' she said. 'You press guys are incredible. How did you know I was here?' she asked.

Phil grinned. 'We were tipped off in a phone call,' he told her. 'Can we have a couple of comments about why you're here – and a few pictures?'

Kimberley sighed but smiled again. 'My visit was supposed to be private; low profile,' she began. 'I wanted to see the place where it all started for me. Sentimental, I know, but when I found out that there was a show on tonight, I just couldn't resist staying to watch. And I'm so glad I did.'

She turned round and smiled straight at me. 'In fact,' she went on, 'the real star of the show tonight was Alex here! She was brilliant – such a natural comedian.'

'Wonderful,' Phil said. 'Alex, what praise coming from Kimberley! Is there anything you would like to add?'

'Well, I'm completely chuffed, of course –' I began, when suddenly a wicked but irresistible idea occurred to me – 'but, Phil, it wouldn't be right if I didn't say thank you to Pearl Barconi, the original Alice, who unfortunately had to drop out at the last minute due to sudden illness.

'Oh dear,' he replied sympathetically. 'What is the poor girl suffering from?'

'A bright orange fake tan, Phil,' I replied solemnly.

Rosie burst out laughing and gave me a thumbs up.

Phil grinned but wrote down *everything* I'd said! 'Right, let's get some photos with Kimberley and the kids, Brian,' he told the photographer. 'This is going to make a great feature, Kimberley – you'll love it, I promise.'

'OK, everyone, gather round Miss Hunter and smile straight into the lens just below that red light on the camera,' Brian ordered.

There wasn't even time to worry about whether my hair was all right or anything!

'Big smile, now. Yeah, great!' said Brian. 'Now, let's have a close-up of Kimberley with Alice and the White Rabbit next . . .'

The camera clicked and whirred so many times I couldn't keep up, but eventually Phil declared that it was 'in the bag'.

'Marvellous!' said Kimberley. She looked at her watch. 'Oops. I think my car will be waiting. Thanks, Phil, I'll look forward to seeing the shots back at my agent's office.

Now,' she turned to the cast, 'I can't believe it's time to go already. You've all been great. It's been such fun to meet you all.' She held out her hand and said goodbye to each of us in turn before heading off to her luxurious film-star hotel.

Rosie grinned at me. 'So, are you glad you went ahead with it now?' she asked.

'Of course!' I replied, grinning back. 'And let's make sure Macaroni gets to read about herself in the spotlight too. I'm going to buy her a personal copy of *Hiya!* next week.'

Rosie grinned back. 'That's rotten,' she said.

'No, darling, that's showbiz,' I said.

Kimberley's Full of Wonder

This week, international film star Kimberley Hunter revisited the place that launched her glittering career: Wonderland Holiday Camp.

Kimberley, who now lives in Hollywood, is in Britain to star in her latest movie, *Revenge is Sweet*, which is currently being filmed near Wonderland.

And it looks as though Wonderland is continuing its tradition of finding new talent: Kimberley praised the performance of young Alex Bond, who stepped in at the last minute as Alice in the holiday camp's production of *Alice in Wonderland*. The two were photographed, along with Alex's best friend, Rosie Stevens, who played the White Rabbit.

So, readers, you heard it here first. Keep an eye out for the comic talents of Alex Bond. We'll expect an exclusive *Hiya!* Celebrity Interview from her when the time comes!

Meanwhile, turn to page 49 for Kimberley Hunter's top beauty tips on how *not* to apply fake tan . . .